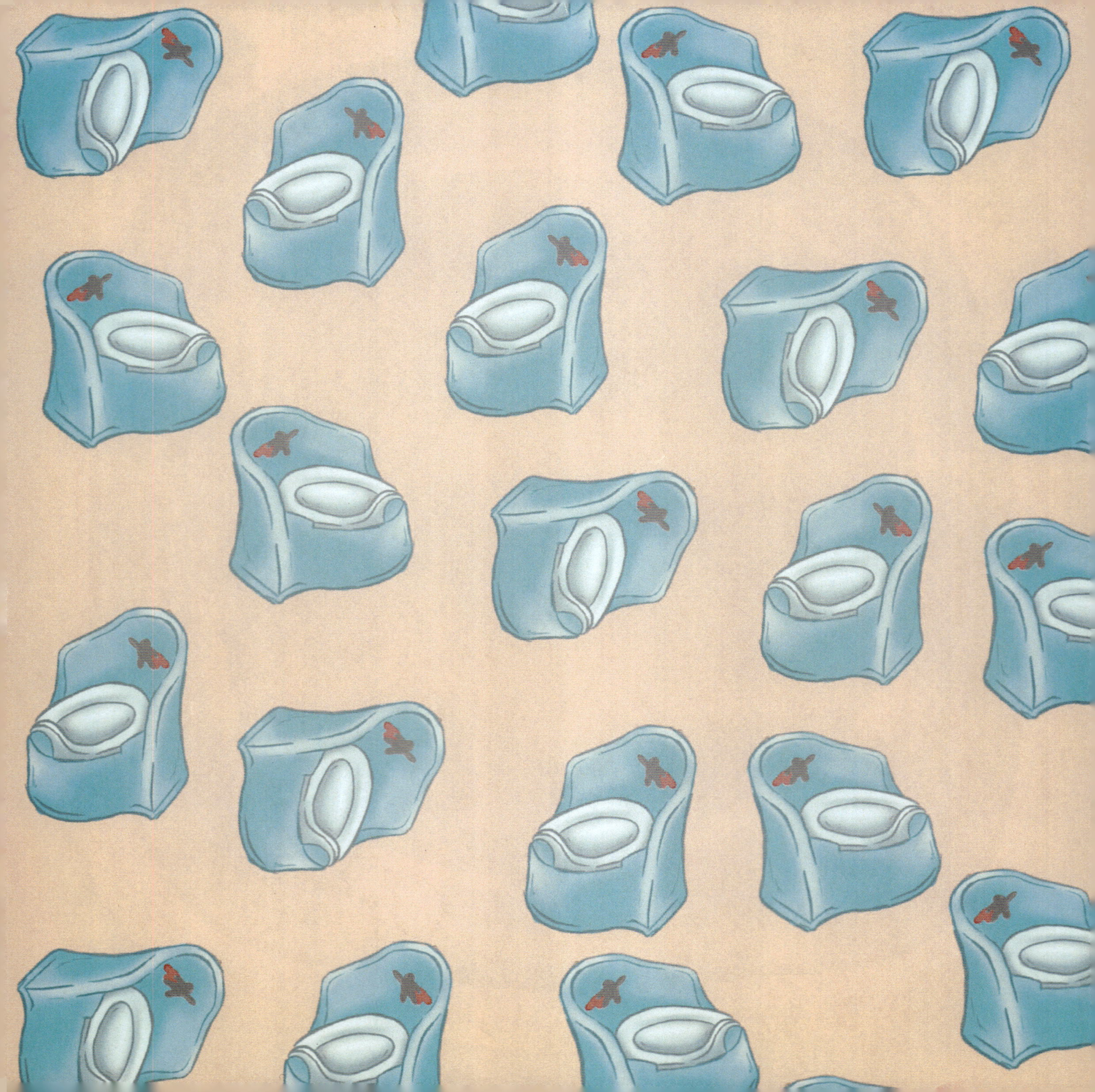

THE BIG BOY POTTY

by Michael Gordon

Go https://michaelgordonclub.wixsite.com/books **to get** "The Grumpy Dinosaur" for **FREE!**

THIS BOOK BELONGS TO

....

....

AGE: ....

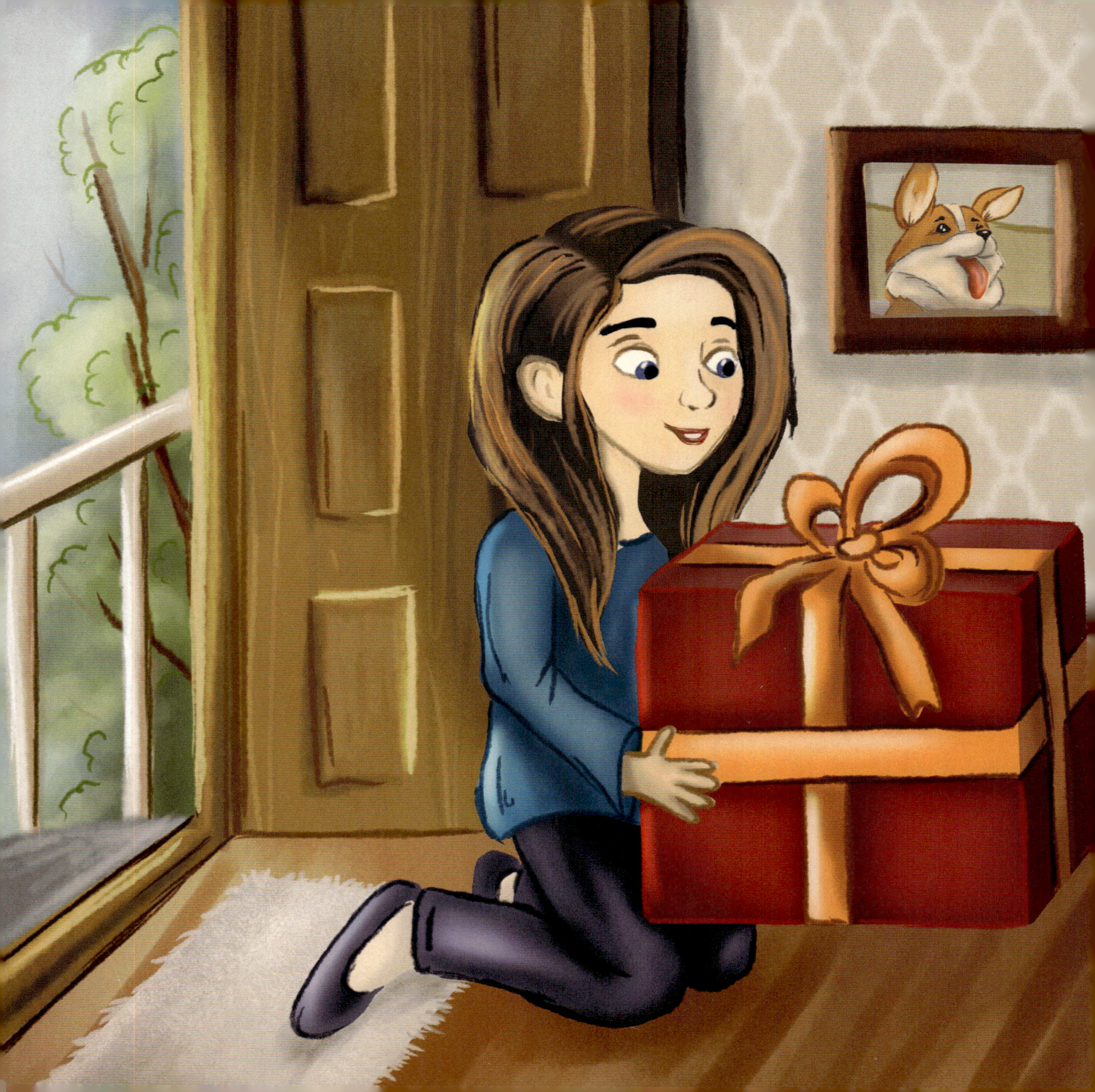

Mom bought Jack a present and brought it home one day.
He was so excited that he put his toys away.
When he unwrapped it, he was delighted to see
Something to sit on—his very own potty!

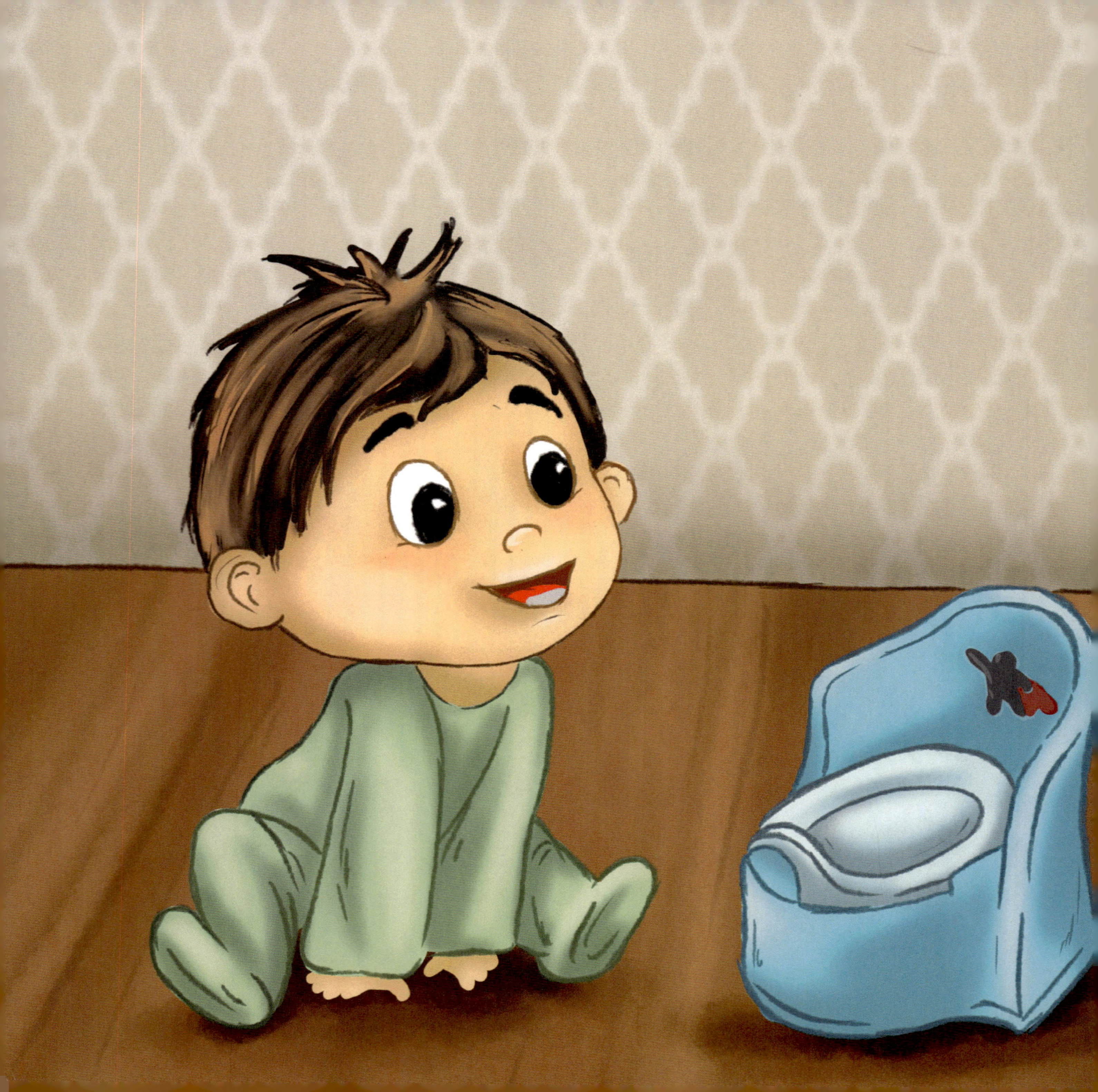

This was no ordinary potty, if you must know.
This one was only for special people to go.
This potty was for superheroes to get the job done.
Jack was a lucky boy to have a special one.

He wanted to get rid of his soggy diapers, you see.
He was as ready for the potty as a big boy could be.
From now on he'd wear big-boy underwear like Dad.
He smiled down at his potty; he was feeling quite glad.

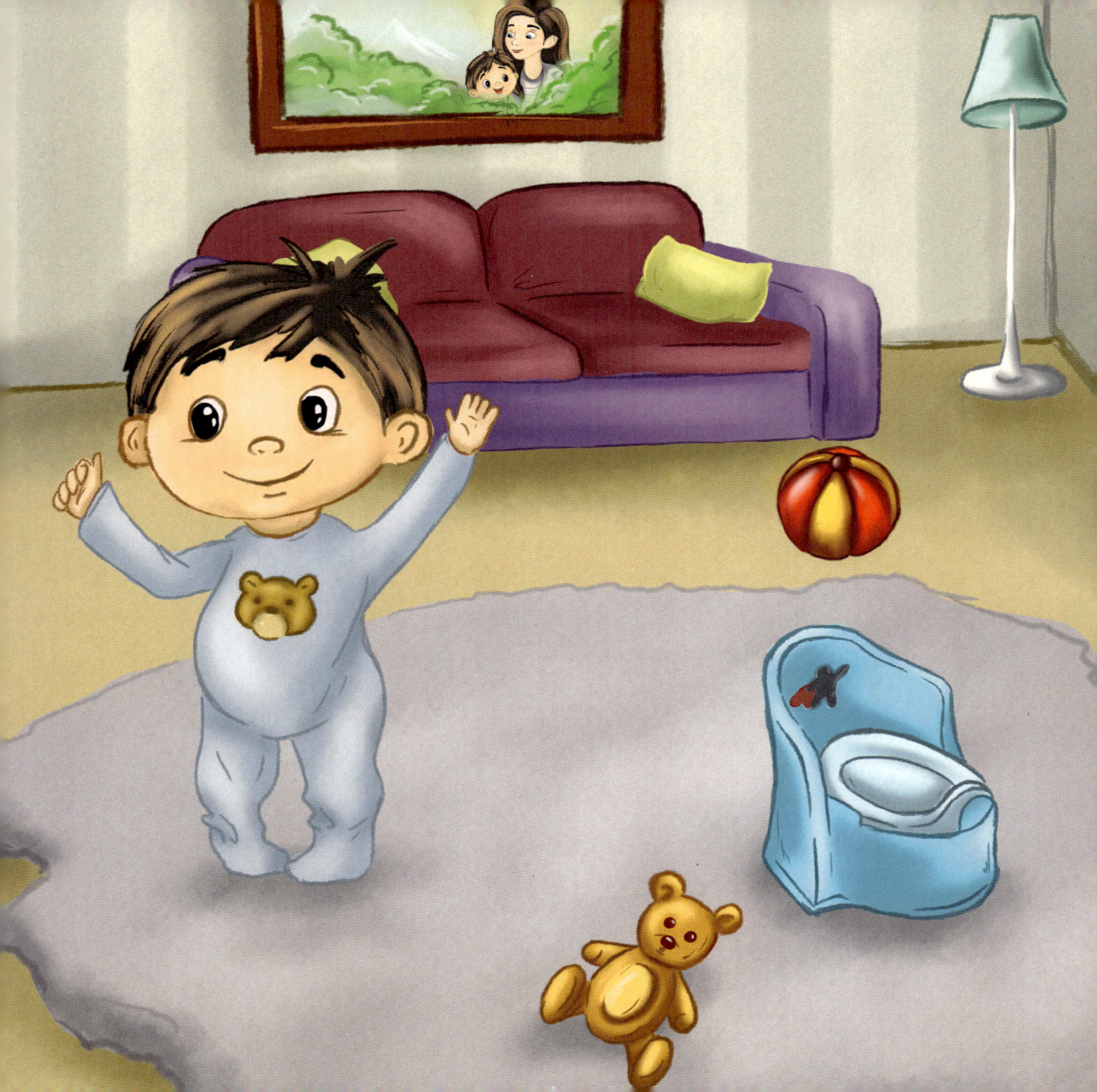

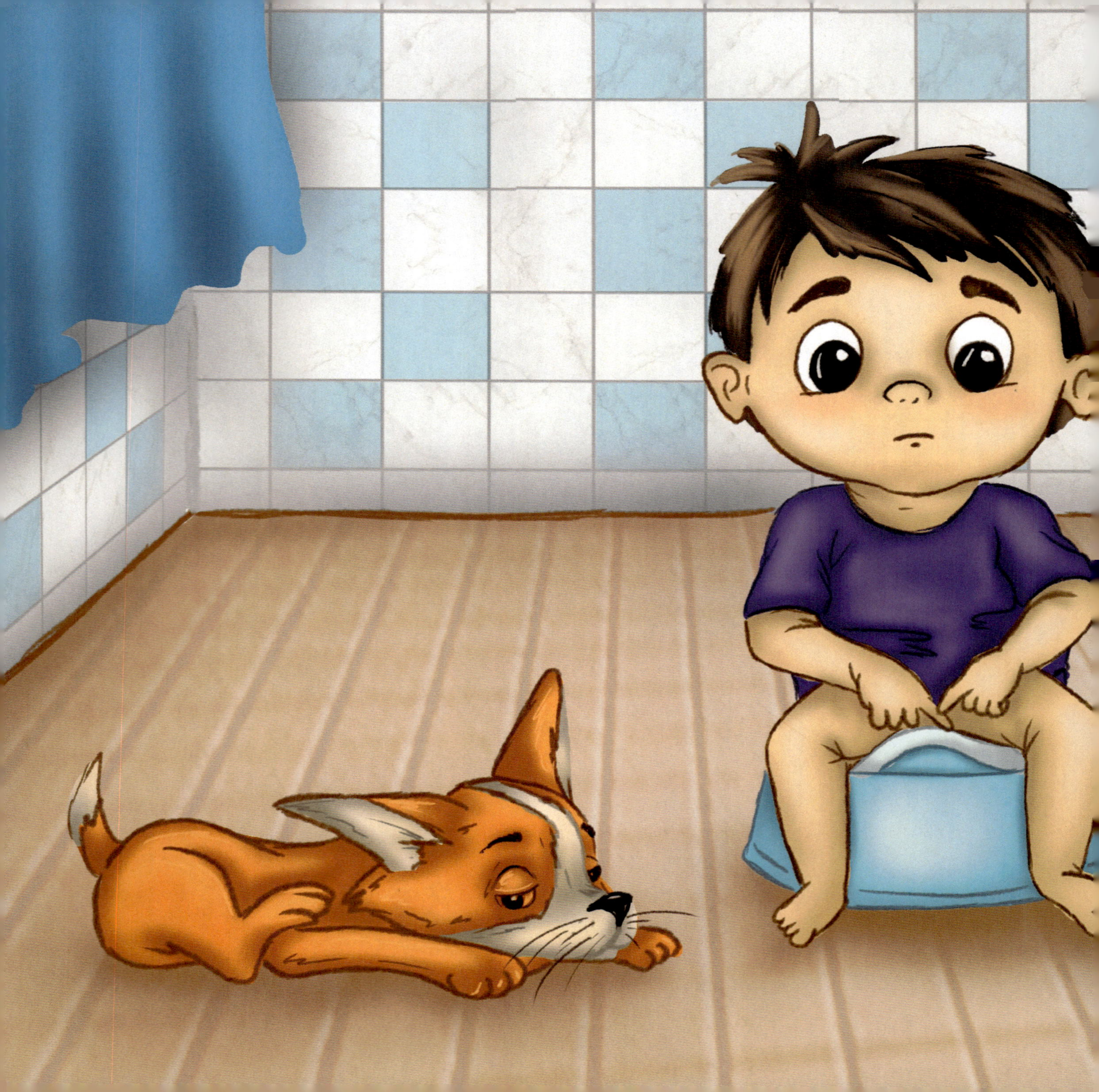

Jack took off his diaper and sat down on the pot.

He waited a while then said, "I almost forgot.

I have stuff to do now, I'll try later today."

Then he jumped off the potty and ran off to play.

The next morning, Jack tried again but nothing came.
So, he got his dog, Benjy, outside to play a game.
The two played together for most of the morning.
Until the rain started to pour down without warning.

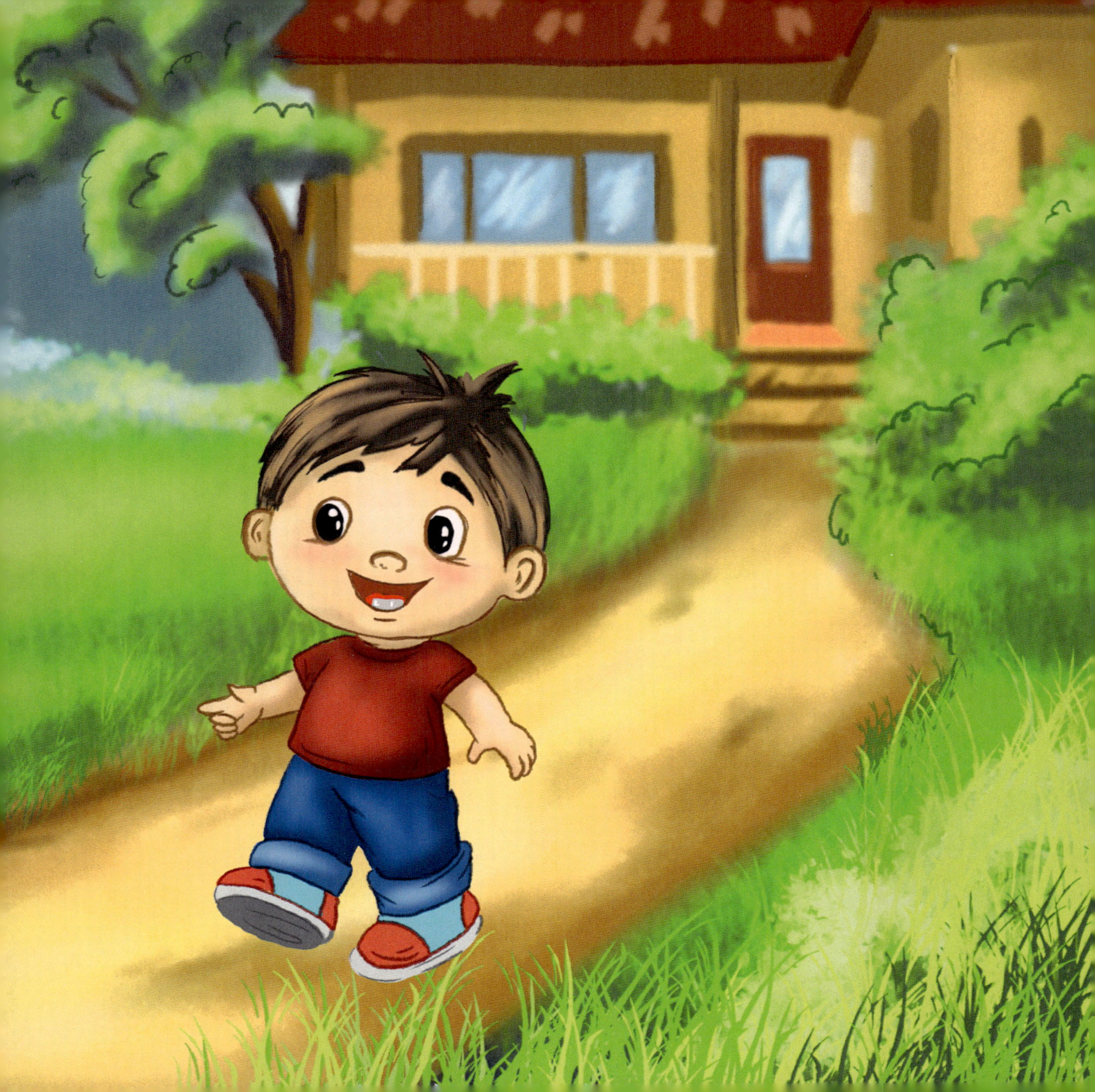

A soaked Jack looked at the potty but decided instead
To take a nice bath; he'd go potty later, before bed.
He played and splashed so hard that he made Benjy run away.
After drying off, he went to find him so they could play.

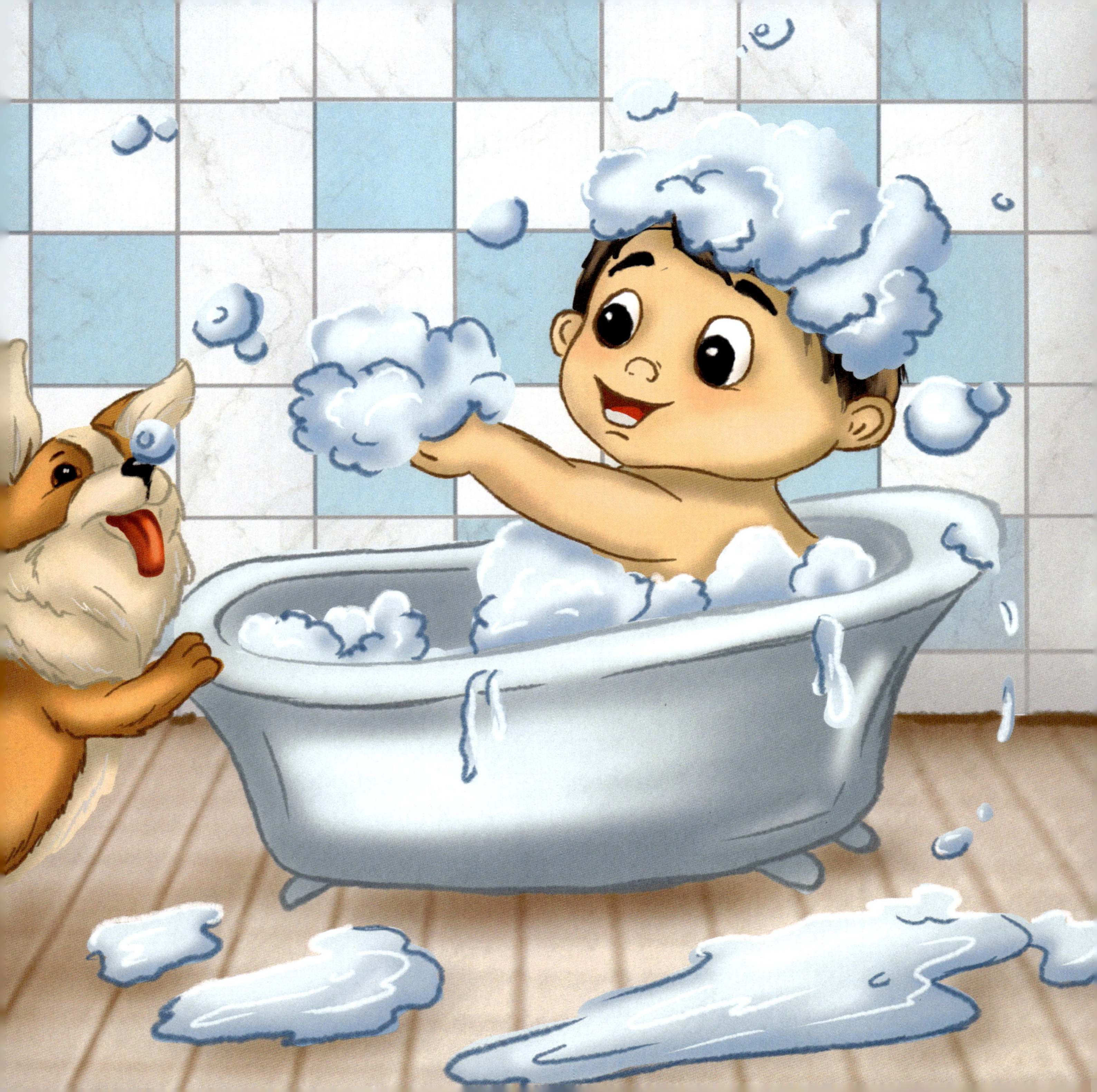

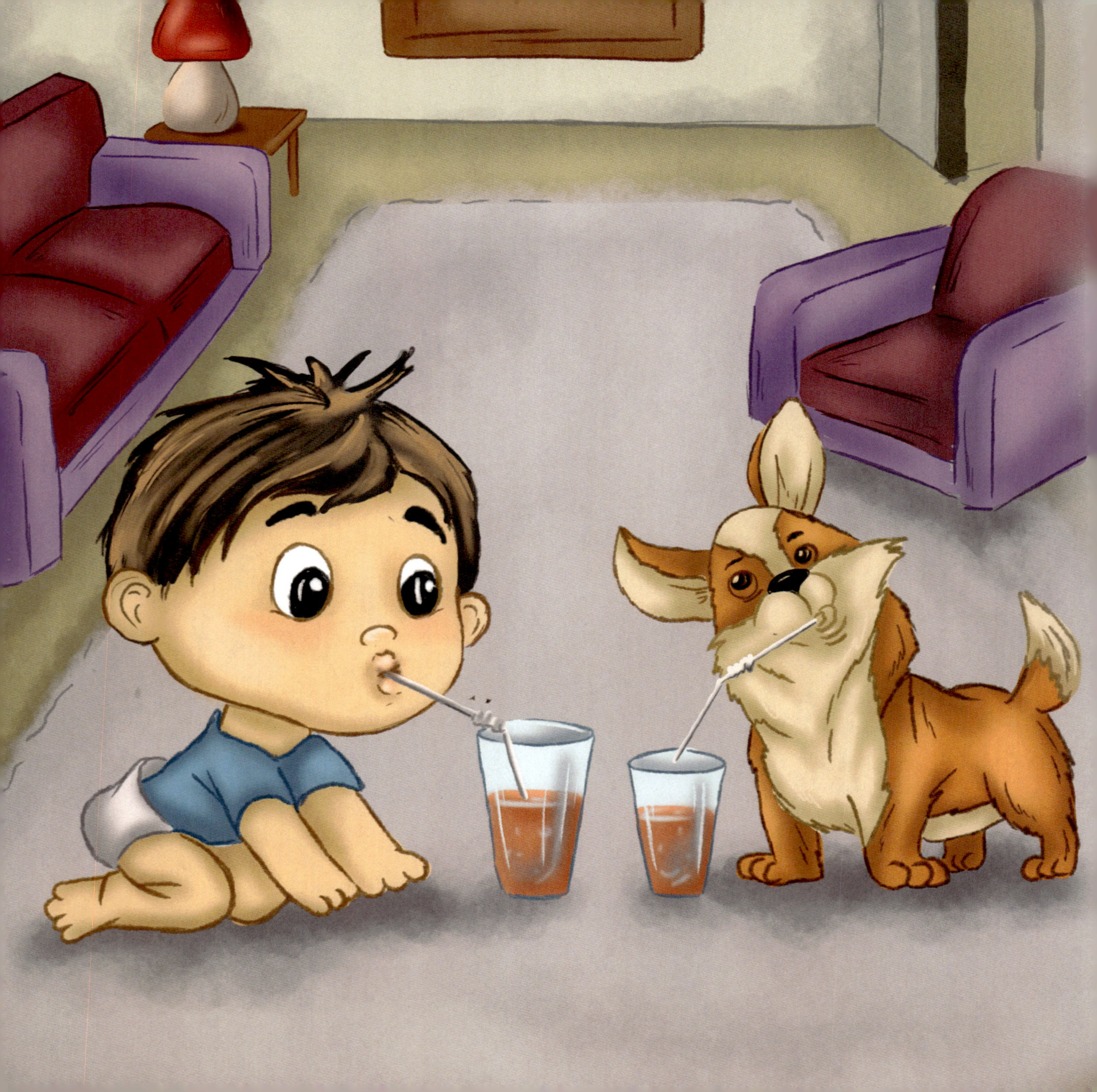

Jack and Benjy played a fun game of hide and go seek.

Jack covered his eyes and made sure not to peek.

After racing around they sat down in the shade.

A thirsty Jack gulped down a big glass of lemonade.

After dinner, Jack felt as full as could be.

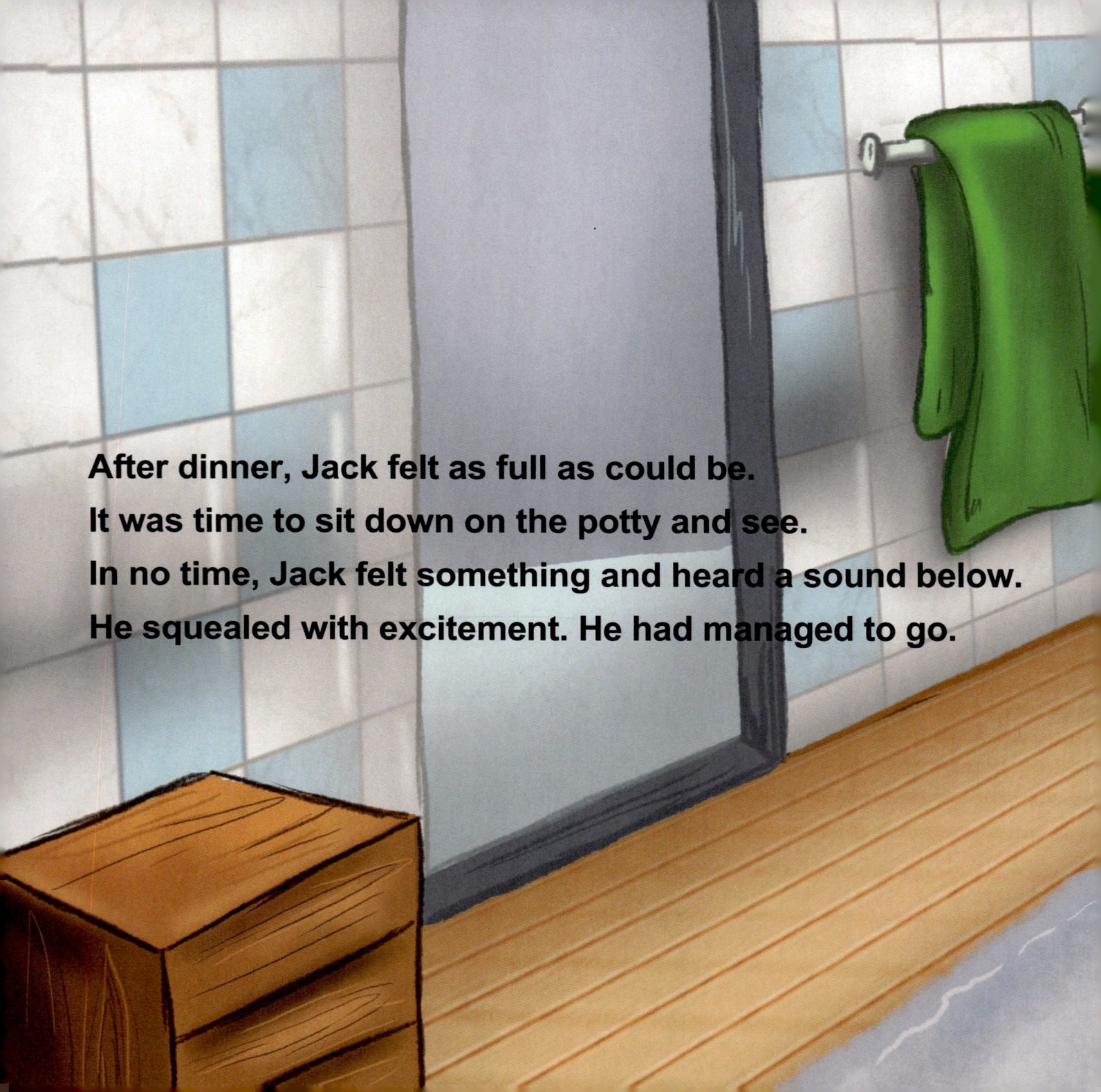

It was time to sit down on the potty and see.

In no time, Jack felt something and heard a sound below.

He squealed with excitement. He had managed to go.

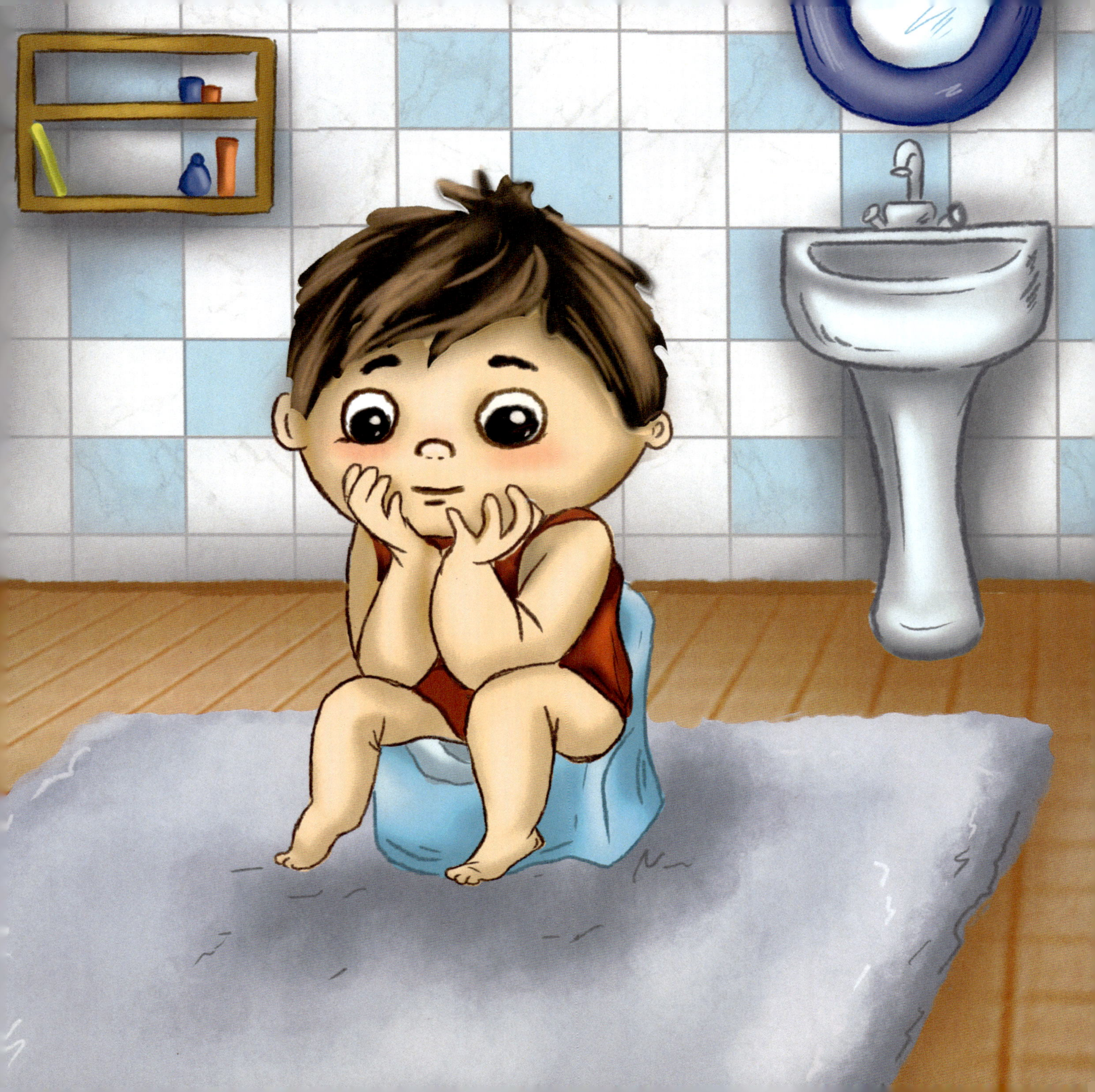

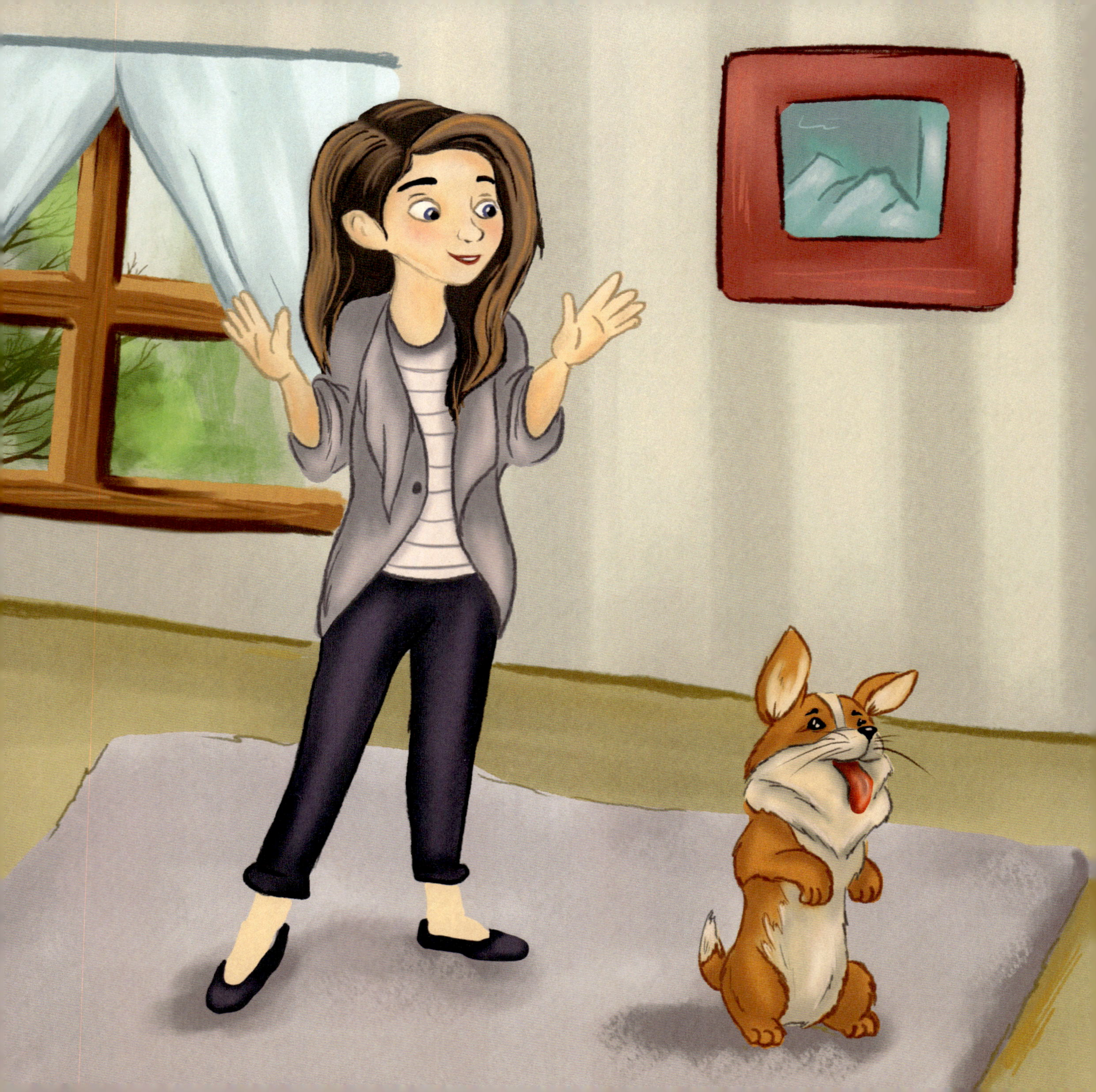

Full of pride, Jack called out, "Mommy, quick, come and see! I did it! I'm a big boy!" His mother agreed.

"I'm so proud of you. I knew you could do it," she said.

Benjy wagged his tail and rubbed Jack's leg with his head.

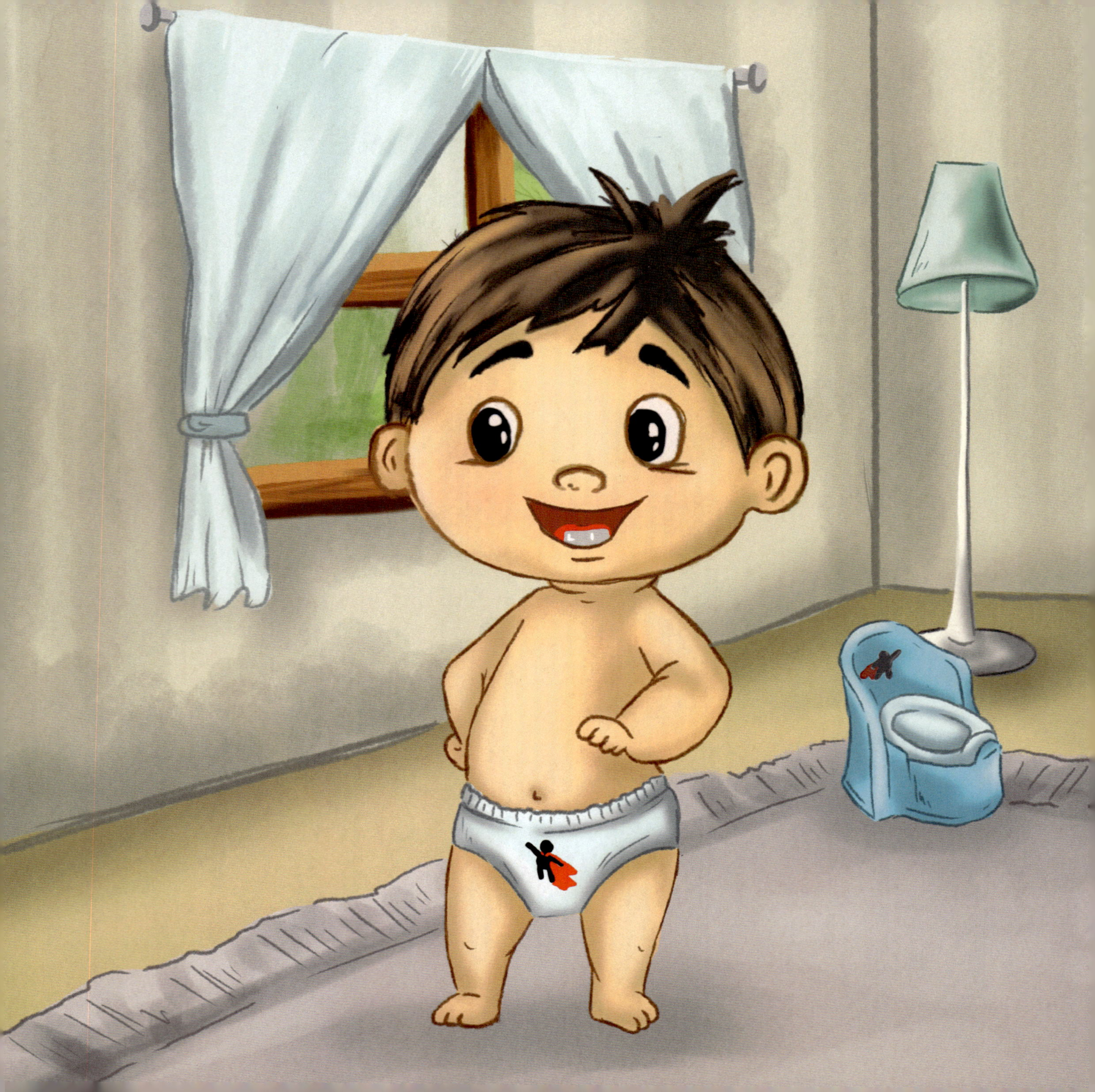

Once Jack was free of diapers, he felt really good.

He wears the kind of underwear a superhero should.

And while saving the world, he often wears two:

One pair under pants and one over—like superheroes do.

THE END

Your opinion could change the word!

I hope you enjoyed this little story.

Reviews from awesome customers like you help other parents to feel confident about choosing this book too.

Would you mind taking a minute to leave your feedback?

I will be forever grateful!

Michael

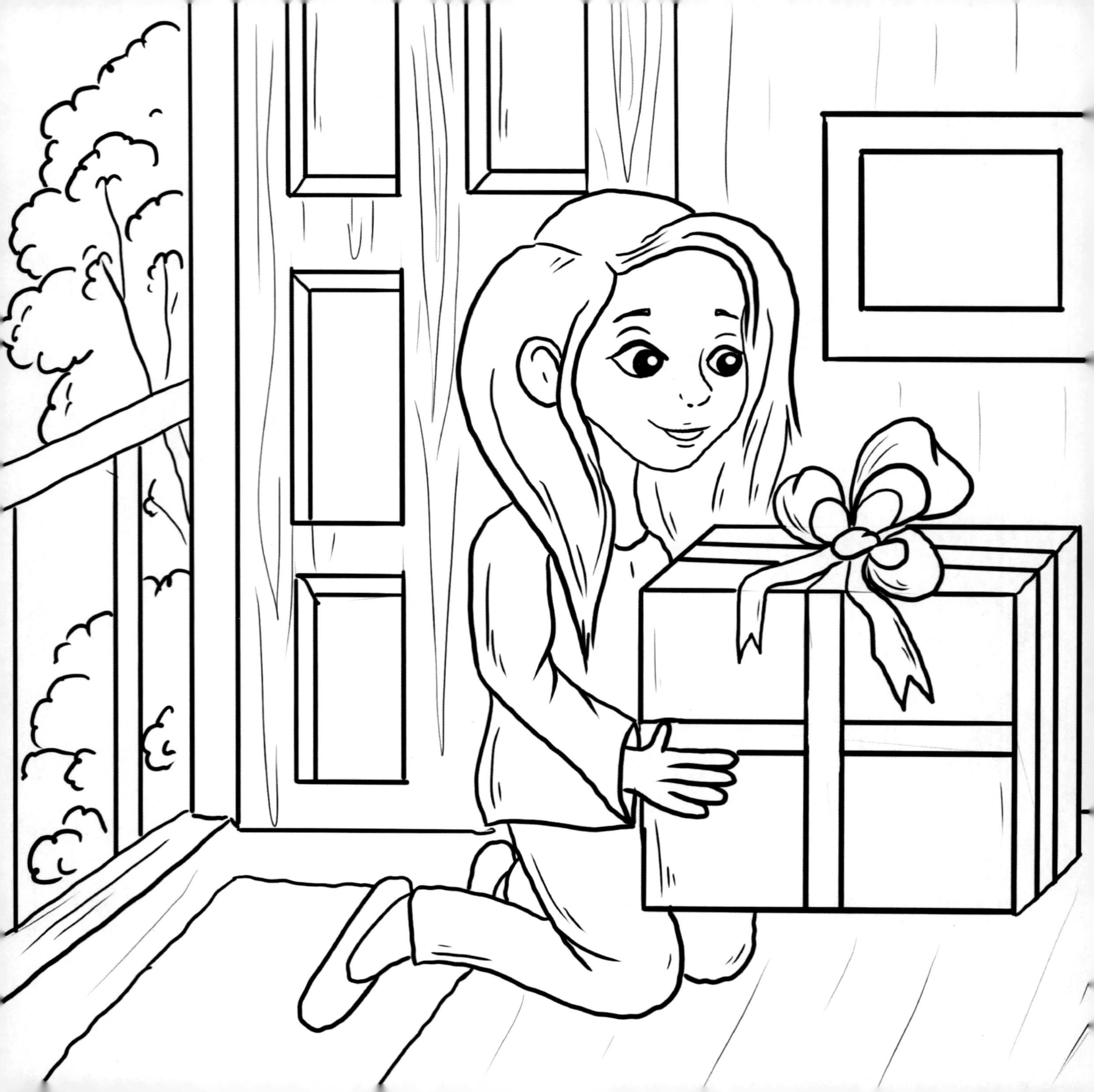

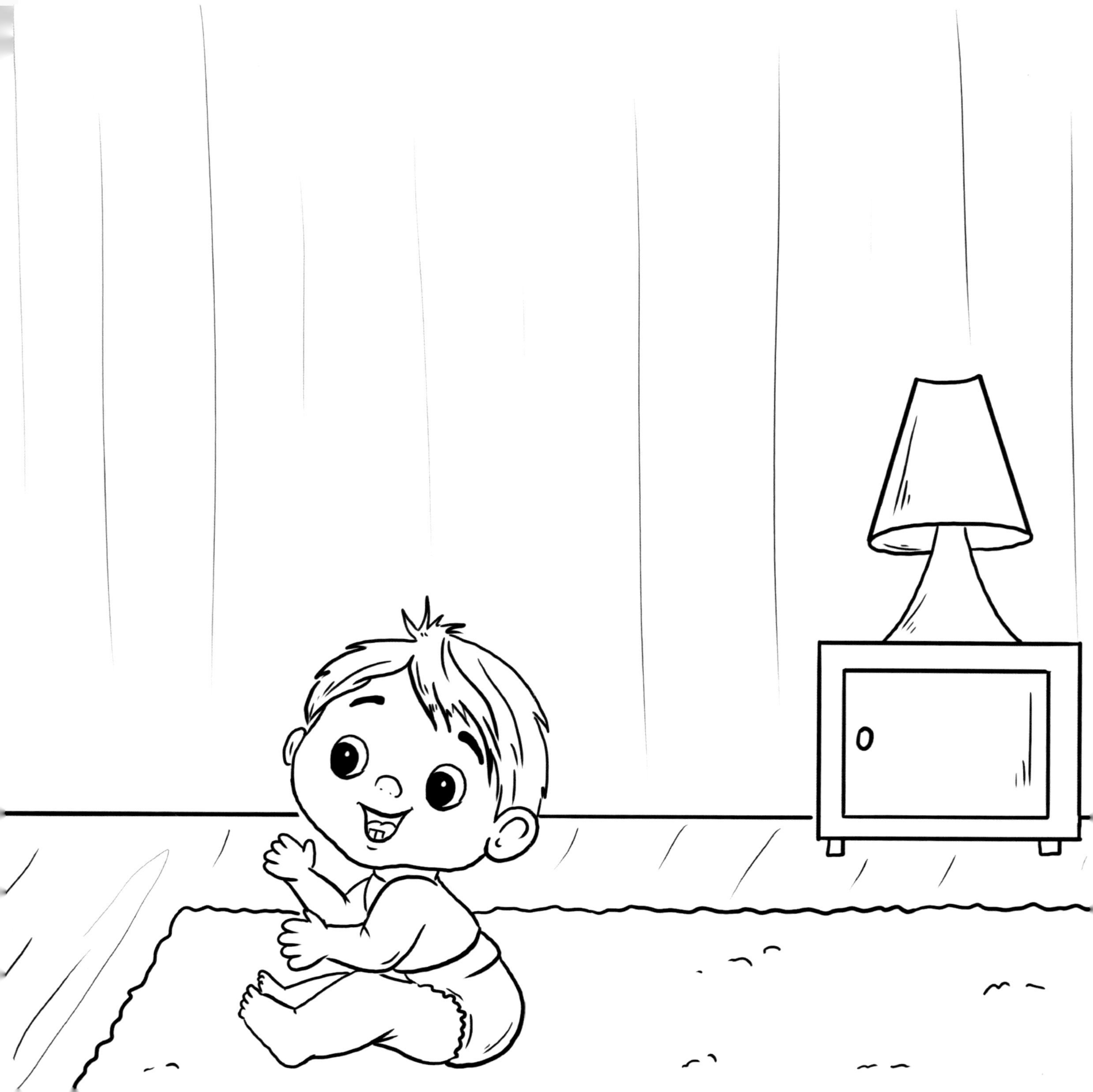

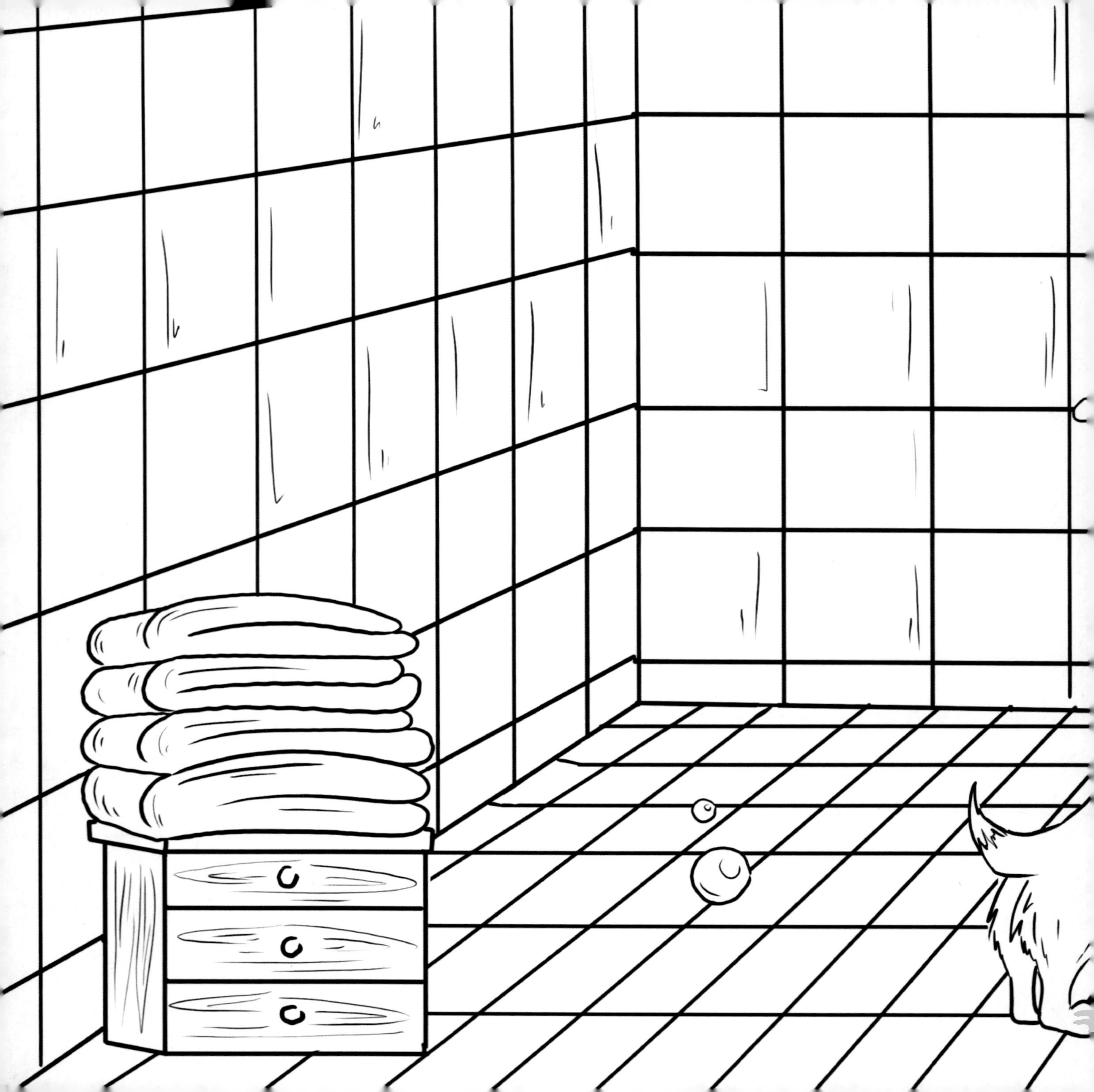

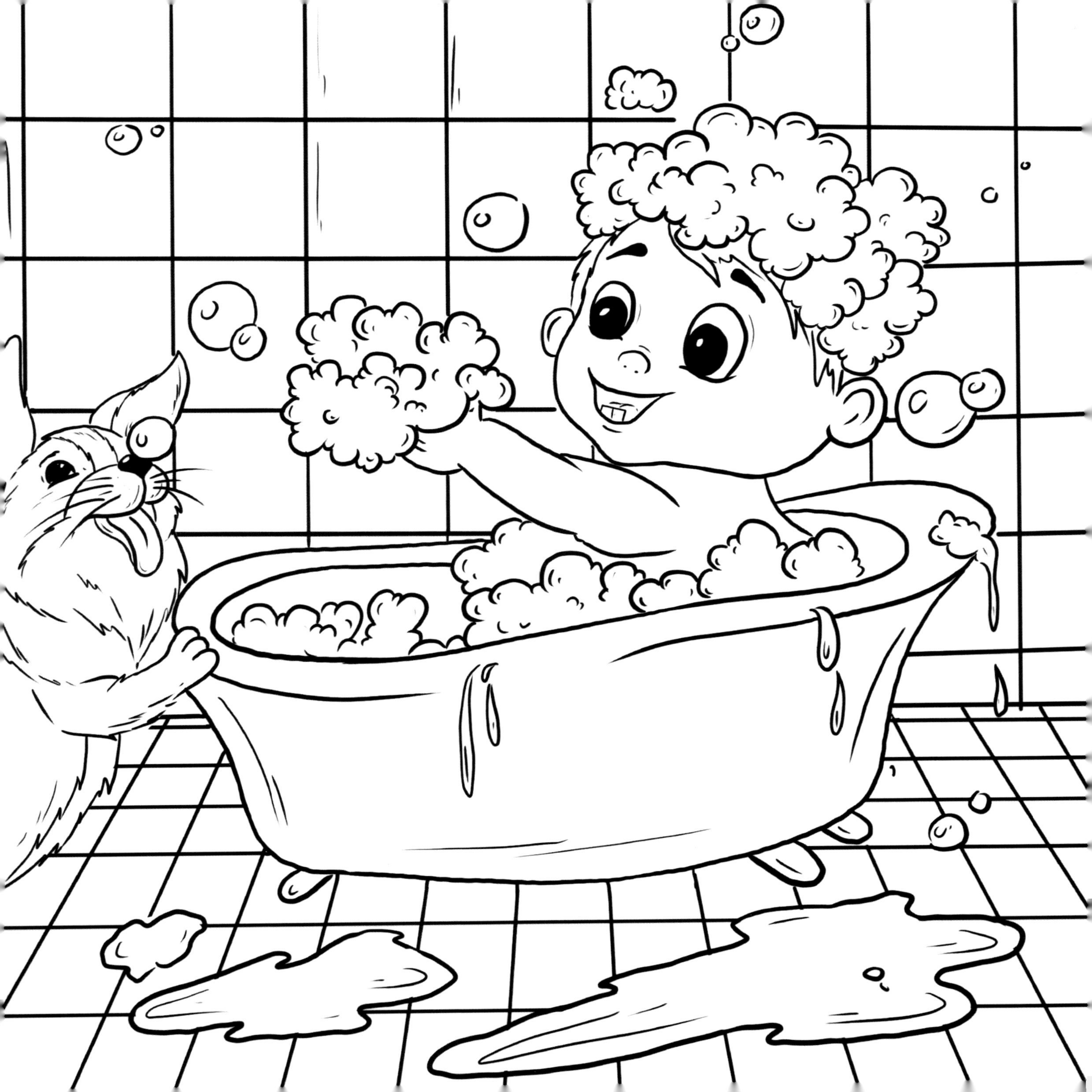

About author

Michael Gordon is the talented author of several highly rated children's books including the popular Sleep Tight, Little Monster, and the Animal Bedtime.

He collaborates with the renowned Kids Book Book that creates picture books for all of ages to enjoy. Michael's goal is to create books that are engaging, funny, and inspirational for children of all ages and their parents.

Contact

For all other questions about books or author, please e-mail michaelgordonclub@gmail.com.

Award-winning books

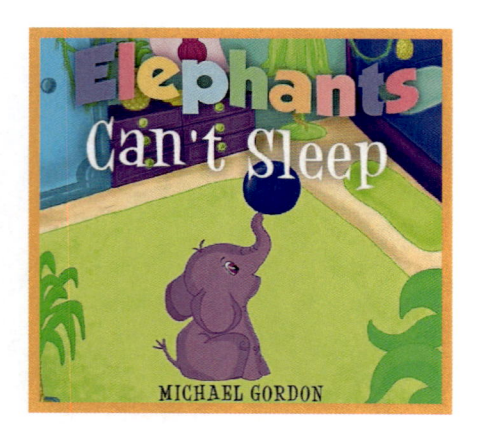

Elephants Can not Sleep

The

Little Elephant likes to break the rules. He never cleans his room. He never listens to mama's bedtime stories and goes to bed really late. But what if he tried to follow the routine so that the bedtime would become an amazing experience?

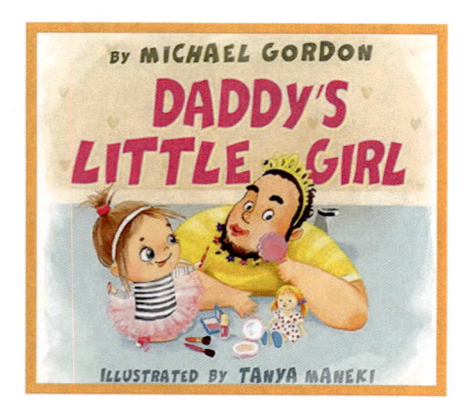

Little Girl's Daddy

the Who Needs a super hero the when you have your dad? Written in beautiful rhyme this is an excellent story that honors all fathers in the world.

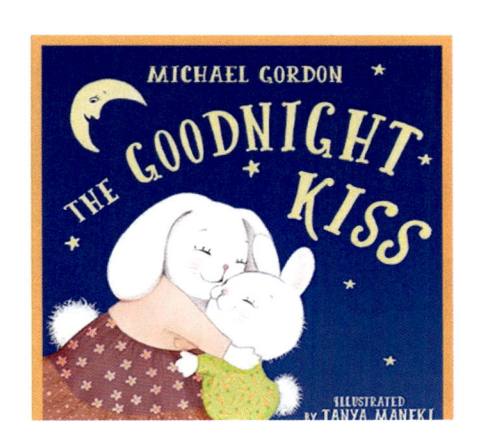

The Goodnight Kiss

Welcome to a cozy, sweet little bunny family. Mom is putting her little son Ben to bed, but she's not quite successful. Little boy still wants to play games and stay up late. Ben also likes to keep his mommy in his room at bedtime. Mrs. Bunny tries milk, warm blankets, books , and finally a kiss ... what will work?

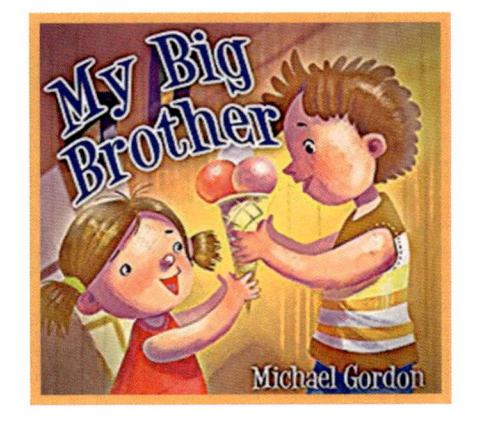

My Big Brother

The

Each of our lives will always be a special part of the other. There's Nothing Quite Like A Sibling Bond Written in beautiful rhyme this is an excellent story that values patience, acceptance and bond between a brother and his sister.

© 2019 Michael Gordon. All rights reserved.

All rights reserved. This book or parts thereof may not be reproduced in any form, stored in any retrieval system, or transmitted in any form by any means—electronic, mechanical, photocopy, recording, or otherwise—without prior written permission of the publisher, except as provided by United States of America copyright law.

Go https://michaelgordonclub.wixsite.com/books **to get** "The Grumpy Dinosaur" for **FREE!**

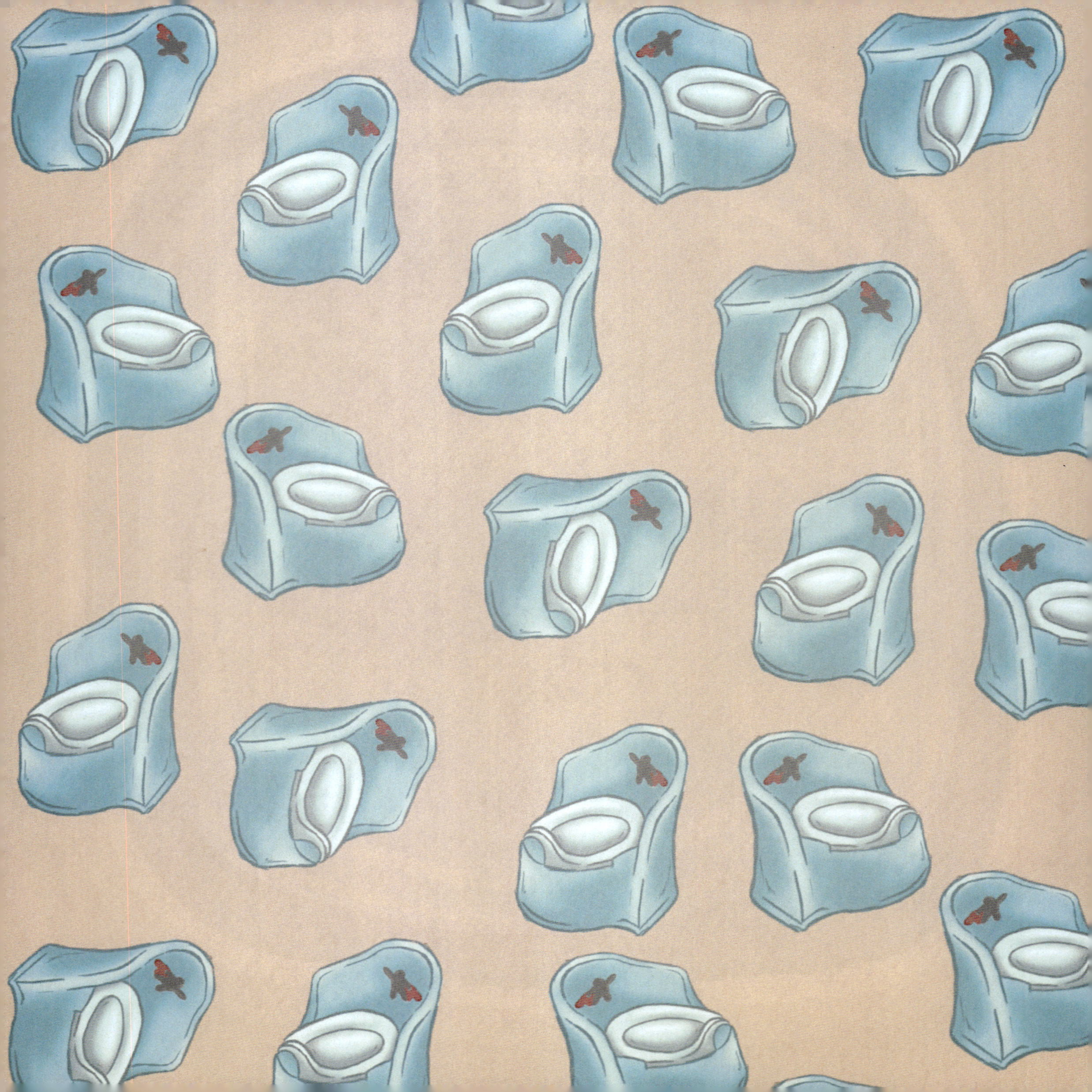

Made in the USA
Middletown, DE
04 December 2022

16967318R00022